I AM PHOENIX

Poems for Two Voices

Also by Paul Fleischman

Picture Books

Time Train
Shadow Play
Rondo in C
The Birthday Tree

Novels

Bull Run
The Borning Room
Saturnalia
Rear-View Mirrors
Path of the Pale Horse
The Half-A-Moon Inn

Short Story Collections

Coming-and-Going Men: *Four Tales*
Graven Images: *Three Stories*

Poetry

Joyful Noise: *Poems for Two Voices*
I Am Phoenix: *Poems for Two Voices*

Nonfiction

Townsend's Warbler
Copier Creations: *Using Copy Machines to Make
Decals, Silhouettes, Flip Books, Films, and Much More!*

I AM PHOENIX

Poems for Two Voices

PAUL FLEISCHMAN

illustrated by Ken Nutt

A Charlotte Zolotow Book

HarperTrophy®
A Division of HarperCollins*Publishers*

Library of Congress Cataloging-in-Publication Data
Fleischman, Paul.
  I am phoenix.
  "A Charlotte Zolotow book."
  Summary: A collection of poems about birds to be read
aloud by two voices.
  1. Birds—Juvenile poetry. 2. Dialogues.
3. Children's poetry, American. [1. Birds—Poetry.
2. American poetry] I. Nutt, Ken, 1951–   ill.
II. Title.
PS3556.L422812   1985   811'.54   85-42615
ISBN 0-06-021881-9
ISBN 0-06-021882-7 (lib. bdg.)
ISBN 0-06-446092-4 (pbk.)

18 19 20 SCP 20 19
Designed by Constance Fogler
First Harper Trophy edition, 1989.

For Charlotte, *rara avis*

CONTENTS

NOTE

The following poems were written to be read aloud by two readers at once, one taking the left-hand part, the other taking the right-hand part. The poems should be read from top to bottom, the two parts meshing as in a musical duet. When both readers have lines at the same horizontal level, those lines are to be spoken simultaneously.

I AM PHOENIX
Poems for Two Voices

Dawn

At first light the finches
are flitting about the trees

        Flittering

fluttering

        flit

purple finches

        flit

Fluttering

        flittering

fly

        painted finches

fly.

        Weaver finch
        goldfinches

Weaver finch

goldfinches

finches

flit

brown-capped rosy finch

flutter

flit

finches.

Cassin's finch

house finches

flit

finches

flit

flutter

flit

flutter

flit

finches.

Morning

One waxwing's wakened

two

two

rails have risen

three

three

teal

four

four

storks

five

five

stilts

six

six

California condors

seven sleek

seven sleek

trumpeter

swans

eight scaups

        nine snipes

ten shrikes

twelve   twelve

        rufous-sided towhees

fifteen   fifteen

magnificent   magnificent

frigatebirds   frigatebirds

twenty terns

        thirty-five

dazzling   dazzling

        lazuli buntings

fifty ruffs

        sixty wrens

seventy-seven

sea gulls   sea gulls

        saviors of

Salt Lake City   Salt Lake City

eighty grouse

        ninety grebes

one hundred   one hundred

chickadees!   chickadees!

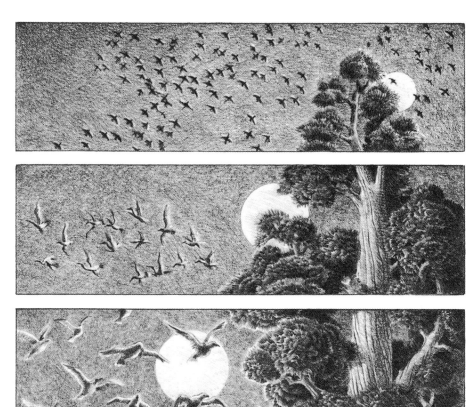

The Wandering Albatross

Behold the wandering
albatross!
Roaming the lonely
oceans

Believed to bear
the souls of lost
mariners

wandering albatross
Men lost to
storms and sharks

Behold the wandering
albatross!

albatross
wandering

wandering
Sailors swept overboard
wandering albatross

albatross roaming

arisen

a-soaring

Albatross!
Wandering
albatross
Wandering
wandering
albatross!

albatross roaming
The shipwrecked

The storm-drowned

Albatross!
Wandering
ceaselessly
journeying

Wandering
albatross!

The Actor

I
seem   seem
                               a shrike

I
ape   ape
                               the gull

I
sing just like   sing just like
                               the cardinal.
                               I
mimic   mimic
coots

                               I
mirror   mirror
crows

imitate
the orioles.
I
copy

I
echo

I know by heart

But all of that

sham

is what
I *am.*

I
imitate

copy
wrens

echo
owls
I know by heart
the catbird's calls.

is simply
sham
For a mockingbird

I *am.*

The Watchers

Overhead vultures fly

Overhead vultures fly

Peregrine falcons fly

Peregrine falcons fly

Pigeon hawks

Pigeon hawks

sparrow hawks

sparrow hawks

red-tailed hawks

red-tailed hawks

sharp-shinned hawks

sharp-shinned hawks

circling

Black hawks

Black hawks

slowly circling

Marsh hawks

Marsh hawks

peering

down

down

ground   at the
                          ground
                          with
great   great
interest.   interest.

The Passenger Pigeon

We were counted not in

thousands

nor

millions

but in
billions.   *billions.*

We were numerous as the

stars   stars

in the heavens

As grains of
sand   sand
at the sea

	As the
buffalo	buffalo
	on the plains.
When we burst into flight	
	we so filled the sky
that the	
sun	sun
was darkened	
	and
day	day
	became dusk.
Humblers of the sun	Humblers of the sun
we were!	we were!
The world	
inconceivable	inconceivable
	without us.
Yet it's 1914,	
and here I am	
alone	alone
	caged in the Cincinnati Zoo,
the last	
	of the passenger pigeons.

The Common Egret

They call us
common
common
egrets.

Common!

The injustice!

As if to be so white that
snow
snow
is filled with envy

clouds
clouds
consumed with spite

that milk
that milk
should seem molasses

rates as ordinary.

Gold	Gold
should be so slandered	
diamonds	diamonds
scorned as worthless	
rubies	rubies
spurned	
	if common
egrets	egrets
	are but
common.	*common.*

The Phoenix

I am Phoenix

Phoenix
everlasting!
I am Phoenix!

Immortal
eternal.
I live in
Arabia

eagle
My feathers are
scarlet,
purple,

I am Phoenix
the fire-bird!
Phoenix

I am Phoenix!
Immortal
eternal
undying.

Arabia
I'm as large as an
eagle

scarlet,

golden.

one

there have never been more.
I am my own
daughter
granddaughter
great-granddaughter
I was

will be
my gravedigger.

I gather up twigs of
sweet-smelling spices
and build a nest
on the top of a palm.

Then I wait for noon—

fire
I flap my wings

purple.
There is but
one
Phoenix—

I am my own
mother
grandmother
great-grandmother.
I was
my own midwife,
will be

For each time I discover
I'm becoming old

sweet-smelling spices

I climb inside.

and when the sun's hot as
fire

burst
into flames

which I fan
with my wings
and fan

and I

Eight days pass.
The ashes cool.

in the morning,

just as the sun

I rise
from the ashes
and fly upward—

new

till the twigs beneath me
burst

which I fan
with my wings
and fan
and fan
till the fire

are no more.

Eight days pass.

Then, on the ninth day

at dawn,

rises in the east
I rise

a
new
Phoenix,

my own

mother	daughter
grandmother	granddaughter
great-grandmother	great-granddaughter
and on	
and on	and on
until the end of time.	until the end of time.

Warblers

Warblers
warbling

Nashville
warblers

Townsend's
Myrtle
Mourning
Wilson's
warblers

Yellow-
throated

Warblers
warbling

Nashville
warblers

Townsend's
Myrtle
Mourning
Wilson's
warblers

Yellow-
throated

Chestnut-
sided

Dozens
of them

Each one
different.

Hooded
warblers

Hermit
warblers

Bachman's
Brewster's
Blue-winged warblers
warbling.

Chestnut-
sided

Dozens
of them

Each one
different.
Hooded
warblers

Hermit
warblers

Bachman's
Brewster's

Blue-winged warblers
warbling.

The Cormorant's Tale

"As free as a bird"

And I choke when I hear it

I'm an old cormorant
That's my man
with the rope

That circles my throat.
Like all cormorants

The skill's in my bones

"As free as a bird"
I've heard my man say

Consider my case.
I'm an old cormorant

Attached to the ring

Like all cormorants
At catching fish I excel

As my owner knows well.

It's a cormorant's life
To dive down—as right now.

I'm a practiced sea-fowl.
But I'm a caught cormorant

And the rings
round our necks

Just to taste is our fate
Though our stomachs
are sore

Then we dive after more.
I'm a cormorant, yes

To be free and unfettered—
As free as a fish.

It's a cormorant's life

I spot a fish and I seize it

But I'm a caught cormorant
—Not the first nor the last—

Stop us eating our catch.
Just to taste is our fate

But *they* take the fish

I'm a cormorant, yes
And I'll tell you my wish:

As free as a fish.

Sparrows

Sparrows everywhere
There's sparrows
everywhere
They're
squabbling
flitting
singing
Sharp-tailed

Henslow's

Lincoln's

Sparrows everywhere
There's sparrows
everywhere
They're
flitting
singing
squabbling

found in marshes

note white eye-ring

fond of thickets

Vesper

white tail feathers
visible while perching.

Sparrows everywhere
They're
flying
chirping
flirting

feeds on insects

sings in flight

bird of brushland

found at dunes from
Cape Cod south to Georgia.
Sparrows
every-
where there's
squabbling
flitting
singing
sparrows

Sparrows everywhere
They're
flirting
flying
chirping
Seaside

Cassin's

Clay-colored

Ipswich

Sparrows
every-
where there's
squabbling
sparrows
flirting

every-
where there's
sparrows
everywhere.

flying
chirping
sparrows
everywhere.

Doves of Dodona

In the country called Greece
We are doves of Dodona

We are doves of Dodona
Near the peak
called Tomarus

All-fathoming birds
All-fathoming birds
Stood the town
called Dodona
Wise doves of Dodona

Wise doves of Dodona
Where our cooing
for thousands of years
has been heard.

We still perch in the oaks
Sacred oaks of Dodona

Sacred oaks of Dodona
Where the oracle lived

In the holy grove
There the prophetess stood
Ancient trees of Dodona

She pondered their questions
We are doves of Dodona

Unpuzzling birds
We answered with cooing
Sage doves of Dodona

We disclosed dying days
Oracle of Dodona

Dweller among trees
Told the outcomes of wars
Priestess of Dodona

In the holy grove

Ancient trees of Dodona
And received those
who sought
what the future might hold.

We are doves of Dodona
Then posed them to us

Unpuzzling birds

Sage doves of Dodona
Which only she knew
how to translate
to words.

Oracle of Dodona
Answered questions of love

Dweller among trees

Priestess of Dodona
Till Dodona
was abandoned
and the questions ceased.

In the country called Greece
We are doves of Dodona

We are doves of Dodona
Near the peak
called Tomarus

All-fathoming birds
Stood the town
called Dodona
Wise doves of Dodona

All-fathoming birds

Wise doves of Dodona
Where our cooing
for thousands of years
has been heard.

Dusk

swifts and swallows
Snapping up insects
swifts and swallows.

Barn swallows
swifts and swallows
Cliff swallows
cave swallows
swifts and swallows

swallows
swift swallows
swift swallows

At dusk there are swallows
swifts and swallows

swifts and swallows.
Barn swallows
bank swallows
swifts and swallows

Cliff swallows
swifts and swallows
Swift and all-swallowing
swallows

swift swallows

swift swallows

swift swallows
swift swallows
swift swallows.

swift swallows
swift swallows
swift swallows.

Whip-poor-will

Whip-poor-will
Will who?
Whip-poor-will

Whip-poor-will
But why?
Whip-poor-will

Whip-poor-will

Hawk told crow
down below

whip-poor-will

Whip-poor-will

Whip-poor-will
Will Grime.
Whip-poor-will

Whip-poor-will
His crime.

He stole a stallion,
witnessed by a hawk high up.

whip-poor-will
Crow told owl
in an oak

Owl told thrush
in a bush

whip-poor-will

Thrush told flea

Flea told dog

Dog told master

Whip

Whip

poor

poor

Will.

Will.

Owls

Sky's dark,

Sun's down,

Larks sleeping
Black night

Loons sleeping

Bright noon
for owls.

Black night
for them,
Bright noon

(siskins sleeping)

Barn owls

(phoebes dreaming)
Screech owls

Barred owls

Screech owls

are

          lis-

          ten-

are   ing

lis-

ten-

ing   are

          lis-

          ten-

          ing

Spotted owls

          (sleeping cranes)

Saw-whet owls

          (dreaming quail)

Elf owls   Elf owls

          are

          call-

          ing

are   out

call-

ing

out   are

          call-

          ing

Great gray owls   Great gray owls
are
calling   calling
out
into the night.   into the night.

Paul Fleischman was born in Monterey, California, and grew up in Santa Monica. He attended the University of California at Berkeley and the University of New Mexico in Albuquerque, and now lives in Pacific Grove, California. He is the author of a number of distinguished books for young readers, including the 1989 Newbery Medal-winning *Joyful Noise: Poems for Two Voices*; the Newbery Honor book *Graven Images*; and *The Half-a-Moon Inn*.

Ken Nutt was born and grew up in Ontario. His work has been represented in several one-man shows there, where he has also received numerous grants and awards for excellence. He is the illustrator of several children's books, including *Joyful Noise: Poems for Two Voices* by Paul Fleischman, under the name of Eric Beddows. He currently lives in Stratford.